To Dust

For in

Love
Erin

FLY BY NIGHT

FLY BY NIGHT

Randall Jarrell

PICTURES BY

MAURICE SENDAK

A Sunburst Book

Farrar, Straus and Giroux

To Mary

FLY BY NIGHT

If you turn right at the last stoplight on New Garden Road and go north for a mile and a half, you
come to a lake on a farm. Beyond, at the edge of the
forest, there is a house with a window seat and a big
willow—the house is covered with ivy, and the ivy is
full of sparrows' nests. If you walk along the edge

of the yard, outside the hedge, a big red chow walks along by you on the inside, barking and wagging his tail. Sometimes there is a cat on the porch, a striped gray one.

A little boy lives there—sometimes you see him sitting in a tree house in the willow. He sits in it so much that the sparrows are used to him, and light just out of reach in the branches. When he takes the cat up with him, though, they sit in the ivy and scold; the cat never stays long.

The boy plays on the lawn with the dog and cat or in the forest with the dog—there aren't any children for him to play with. In the middle of the afternoon he goes and stands by the mailbox, so that the mailman can hand the mail to him instead of putting it in the box. But sometimes he stays in his tree house and waves, and the mailman waves back from his car. Sometimes the mailman hears him calling, "Here Reddy! Here Reddy!" to the dog. The cat's name is Flour, the boy's name is David.

At night David can fly.

In the daytime he can't. In the daytime he doesn't even remember that he can. But at night, after his mother has put him to bed, he wakes up, sometimes.

He can't tell how late it is. There isn't a sound. Part of the bed is dark and shadowy, and the rest is white with moonlight. He looks out into the moonlight. Then he stretches his legs out as far as they will go, with the feet together. He can feel the sheet and the blanket and the counterpane pushing down against his toes. He presses his hands against the sides of his legs, with the fingers together, and stretches his head back as far as it will go. Then he takes a deep slow breath, and shuts his eyes and holds his breath; and after a minute he feels himself float up from the bed. He is flying.

It isn't flying exactly, but floating—he floats in the air. He floats feet first, on his back; when he wants to turn he tilts his feet over to the side. Now he tilts his feet to the left and floats out into the hall. He thinks, "Why do I always forget? I always forget. If I remembered in the daytime I could fly in

5

the daytime. All I have to do is remember."

He says to himself, "This time I'll remember."

He comes to his mother's and father's bedroom, and floats in over them. His father is a big mound under the blanket, with his head sticking out at the top. His mother is a medium-sized mound, but where her head should be there's nothing but a pillow—she's put the pillow over her head to help herself go to sleep.

His father and mother are dreaming: he can see their dreams. Just over his father's head it's round and yellow and warm, like firelight, and his father, looking very small, is running back and forth with David on his back, only David is as big as ever. His father is panting. His mother is dreaming she is making pancakes: she pours them out, and turns them over, and piles them in a pile on a plate. Her dream is round and yellow too, but it has got mixed up with the pillow, so that the feathers the pillow is stuffed with float through her dream like snow-flakes.

6

David floats away from them into the living room. The moonlight comes through the windows and makes a big white patch on the floor. Reddy is asleep in it. He is dreaming, too, but it's hard to see his dream: there is something furry, like a squirrel or a rabbit, that he's running after, and his feet twitch and his tail jerks and his tongue hangs out of his mouth—every once in a while he gulps.

David thinks, "They're all asleep but me." He floats to the door of the house. The door opens for him, and he floats through the top of the doorway out onto the porch. Somebody has left a pillow on the porch swing, and the cat is sitting on the pillow, looking out into the yard. His paws are folded under his chest; you can't see his stripes or the white under his chin, it is so dark, but his eyes glow. He says to David:

Wake by night and fly by night,
The wood is black, the wood is white,
The mice are dancing in the moonlight.

And when David looks out to where the cat is looking, by the big oak at the side of the lawn, he sees three mice. They aren't dancing, though; they are running around and around in a circle. He thinks, "Maybe that's the way mice dance."

He floats toward them. When his shadow touches them they all stand still, and one says to the others:

What's that great big black thing in the sky?

One of the others says:

It's little David—he can fly.

Then they see the cat, that has come padding out into the yard behind David, and they all run into the hole at the bottom of the tree and call back over their shoulders:

It's time to go—goodbye, goodbye!

David starts to say to the cat, "They're afraid of you," but he can't say a word; and when he tries to reach down to the cat and pat him, he can't move his arm.

He floats toward the vegetable garden in the back yard. Nothing is its own color: the moonlight makes each row of vegetables look like a long white stripe, and beside it is a black stripe, its shadow. The whole garden is striped black and white. At the farthest end of the farthest row there is a gray something. It hops from that row to the next, and then stops. As David floats over it he can see it is a rabbit. Everything is so still that David can hear the little crunching noise the rabbit makes as it chews.

The rabbit looks up and says:

A squash for me, a beet for you,
A beet for me, a squash for you,
A carrot more and I am through,
One radish more and I am through.

And it runs off with the radish in its mouth.

"Wait! Wait!" David tries to say, but he can't. He floats after the rabbit. After a minute he can't see the rabbit any more, but only its white tail bobbing up and down in the middle of the trees.

13

Then the tail is gone too.

David floats on till he comes to the fence at the edge of the farm. On the other side are six woolly gray mounds the size of the mound his mother makes in the bed. They are the sheep—they are standing there fast asleep. David thinks, "I'll see what they're dreaming." All of them except one are dreaming they're eating; that one is dreaming he's asleep.

Over on the other side of them are three ponies, a big black and white one and two little furry ones, brown, almost black; one of them has a star on his forehead. When they see David the big one whinnies at him. David thinks, "I'll pet him." But when he floats down close to them they are afraid of him, and trot off toward the barn.

David doesn't know what to do. He floats a little higher. On one side of him the field stretches off white in the moonlight, cold and lonely, with nothing on it but the humps the sheep make; he thinks, "It looks like snow." On the other side the forest

14

rises high over him; at its edge he can see white limbs and black shadows, but back inside all of it is black. Up over his head the white moon makes the black sky gray.

Something is coming to David through the air. It glides toward him silently—then it gives two big slow strokes of its wings, but not a single feather makes a sound. It floats around and around David in circles; sometimes it comes so close to him it almost brushes him with its wings. Its wings are wider than his arms. It looks at him with its big round brown eyes: each of them has a feathery white ring around it, and then a brown one, and then a white one, and then a brown one, till the rings come together and make big brown and white rings around its whole head. There are sharp brown stripes on its whitey-brown breast, and its brown wings and brown tail are all barred with white bars. Its beak is bright yellow, and in its claws it is holding a big silvery fish. David thinks, "I didn't know owls could catch *fish*."

The owl floats along by David, and says to him in such a low deep voice it is almost like hearing it inside his head:

My nest is in the hollow tree,
My hungry nestlings wait for me.
I've fished all night along the lake,
And all for my white nestlings' sake.
Come, little nestling, you shall be
An owl till morning—you shall see
The owl's white world, till you awake
All warm in your warm bed, at daybreak.

And David floats after the owl. Whenever the owl gets too far ahead it flies back and glides around and around him. As it looks at him its eyes glow; the fish in its claws shines in the moonlight like a spoon.

They fly out over the edge of the lake. Where the stream runs into it the ducks are floating, five white ones and two dark ones. Then David and the owl come to an oak. The oak is dead at the top, with a hollow in the trunk—on the edge of the hollow are sitting two baby owls. As soon as they see the big owl they open their mouths wide, stand on tiptoe, and flap their wings.

David thinks, "Why, they *are* white!" The little owls have big eyes and big beaks and big dark shadows around their eyes, and are covered from head to foot with white curly down—they look as if somebody had poured handfuls of white wood-shavings over them, or as if they had stayed outside all winter and had got covered with patches of wet snow. And when they have gobbled up the fish and sit by each other again, instead of looking beautiful, like puppies or kittens, they have a sad absurd look, as if they were sitting there waiting for their real feathers to come. But when the big owl turns its head toward them its eyes look loving—David thinks, "It doesn't know the way they look."

The little owls could barely finish the fish, it was so big; now they sit blinking sleepily, and David starts to yawn, but he can't. The big owl sits by the little ones, and softly tells them

THE OWL'S BEDTIME STORY

There was once upon a time a little owl.
He lived with his mother in a hollow tree.
On winter nights he'd hear the foxes howl,
He'd hear his mother call, and he would see
The moonlight glittering upon the snow.
How many times he wished for company
As he sat there alone! He'd stand on tiptoe,
Staring across the forest for his mother,
And hear her far away; he'd look below
And see the rabbits playing with each other
And see the ducks together on the lake
And wish that he'd a sister or a brother.
Sometimes it seemed to him his heart would break.
The hours went by, slow, dreary, wearisome,
And he would watch, and sleep a while, and wake—
"Come home! Come home!" he'd think; and she
     would come
At last, and bring him food, and they would sleep.

Outside the day glared, and the troublesome
Sounds of the light, the shouts and caws that keep
An owl awake, went on; and, dark in daylight,
The owl and owlet nestled there.

                                  But one day, deep
In his dark dream, warm, still, he saw a white
Bird flying to him over the white wood.
The great owl's wings were wide, his beak was
    bright.
He whispered to the owlet: "You have been good
A long time now, and waited all alone
Night after long night. We have understood;
And you shall have a sister of your own,
A friend to play with, if, now, you will fly
From your dark nest into the harsh unknown
World the sun lights."

                            Down from the bright sky
The light fell, when at last the owlet woke.
Far, far away he heard an owlet cry.
The sunlight blazed upon a broken oak
Over the lake, and as he saw the tree

It seemed to the owlet that the sunlight spoke.
He heard it whisper, "Come to me! O come to me!"

The world outside was cold and hard and bare;
But at last the owlet, flapping desperately,
Flung himself out upon the naked air
And lurched and staggered to the nearest limb
Of the next tree. How good it felt to him,
That solid branch! And, there in that green pine,
How calm it was, how shadowy and dim!

But once again he flapped into the sunshine—
Through all the tumult of the unfriendly day,
Tree by tree by tree, along the shoreline
Of the white lake, he made his clumsy way.

At the bottom of the oak he saw a dead
Owl in the snow. He flew to where it lay
All cold and still; he looked at it in dread.
Then something gave a miserable cry—
There in the oak's nest, far above his head,
An owlet sat. He thought: The nest's too high,

I'll never reach it. "Come here!" he called.

"Come here!"

But the owlet hid. And so he had to try
To fly up—and at last, when he was near
And stopped, all panting, underneath the nest
And she gazed down at him, her face looked dear
As his own sister's, it was the happiest
Hour of his life.

In a little, when the two
Had made friends, they started home. He did his best
To help her: lurching and staggering, she flew
From branch to branch, and he flapped at her side.
The sun shone, dogs barked, boys shouted—

on they flew.

Sometimes they'd rest; sometimes they would glide
A long way, from a high tree to a low,
So smoothly—and they'd feel so satisfied,
So grown-up! Then, all black against the snow,
Some crows came cawing, ugly things! The wise
Owlets sat still as mice; when one big crow
Sailed by, a branch away, they shut their eyes

And looked like lumps of snow. And when the night,
The friend of owls, had come, they saw the moon rise.
And there came flying to them through the
     moonlight
The mother owl. How strong, how good, how dear
She did look! "Mother!" they called in their delight.

Then the three sat there just as we sit here,
And nestled close, and talked—at last they flew
Home to the nest. All night the mother would appear
And disappear, with good things; and the two
Would eat and eat and eat, and then they'd play.
But when the mother came, the mother knew
How tired they were. "Soon it will be day
And time for every owl to be in his nest,"
She said to them tenderly; and they
Felt they were tired, and went to her to rest.
She opened her wings, they nestled to her breast.

And when the owl finishes, the little owls—they can hardly keep their eyes open—scramble down into the nest inside the hollow of the oak. David's eyelids are heavy, and yet they won't close, they won't blink, even. The owl leaps into the air and with two big silent strokes of its wings sails away; and when David floats after it, the owl glides around and around him, as they fly over the forest towards David's house.

When they come to the house the owl sails up to David and tilts its wings so that it stops still in the air; then it looks at David with its shining eyes, almost the way it had looked at the owlets, and flies away. David thinks, "The owl looks at me like—"

But he can't think. He floats through the door, down the hall, into his own room; night is ending, and the white of the moonlight and the black of the shadows are beginning to be gray. The sheet and the blanket and the counterpane are heavy on him: he starts to fall asleep, and he can fall asleep.

Then he doesn't know anything; then all at once

he opens his eyes and the sunlight blinds him—he tries to shut them, and they shut, and he can hear birds in the yard and his mother in the kitchen. He jumps up and runs to the kitchen, and his mother swings him up into her arms and kisses him and says, "Little sleepyhead, it's almost nine!" He says, "I slept so late because I—because I—"

His mother says, "Because you what?"

David says, "Because I—there was something I—"

"Here's something for you to drink, and in two shakes of a lamb's tail I'll have some pancakes ready for you to eat," his mother says, and she looks at him like—

"Like—" thinks David, "like—"

He can remember, he can almost remember; but the sunlight streams in through the windows, he holds his hand out for the orange juice, and his mother looks at him like his mother.